RAINBOW magic ®

The Weather Fairies

Join the **Rainbow Magic Reading Challenge!**

Read the story and collect your fairy points to climb the
Reading Rainbow at the back of the book.

This book is worth 5 points.

To Abby and Becky French
– with lots of love

Special thanks to
Sue Mongredien

ORCHARD BOOKS

First published in Great Britain in 2004 by Orchard Books
This edition published in 2016 by The Watts Publishing Group

25

© 2016 Rainbow Magic Limited.
© 2016 HIT Entertainment Limited.
Illustrations © Georgie Ripper 2004

HiT entertainment

A CIP catalogue record for this book is available from the British Library.

ISBN 978 1 84362 637 4

Printed and bound by CPI Group UK Ltd, Croydon, CR0 4YY

MIX
Paper from
responsible sources
FSC® C104740
FSC
www.fsc.org

The paper and board used in this book are made from wood from responsible sources

Orchard Books
An imprint of Hachette Children's Group
Part of The Watts Publishing Group Limited
Carmelite House, 50 Victoria Embankment, London EC4Y 0DZ

An Hachette UK Company
www.hachette.co.uk
www.hachettechildrens.co.uk

Storm
the Lightning
Fairy

by Daisy Meadows

illustrated by Georgie Ripper

ORCHARD

Goblins green and goblins small,
I cast this spell to make you tall.
As high as the palace you shall grow.
My icy magic makes it so.

Then steal Doodle's magic feathers,
Used by the fairies to make all weathers.
Climate chaos I have planned
On Earth, and here, in Fairyland!

Contents

Magic in the Air

"I can't believe tomorrow is my last day here," groaned Rachel Walker. She was staying for a week's holiday with her friend, Kirsty Tate, at the Tates' house in Wetherbury. The girls had had so many adventures together, they knew it was going to be difficult to say goodbye.

They were walking to the park, keen to get outside now the rain had stopped. It had been pouring down all night, but now the sun was shining.

"Put your coats on, though, won't you?" Mrs Tate had told them before they set off. "It looks quite breezy out there."

"It's been such fun, having you to
stay," Kirsty told her friend.
"I don't think I'll ever forget
this week, will you?"

Rachel shook her
head. "No way,"
she agreed firmly.

The two friends smiled
at each other. It had been
a very busy week. A snowy,
windy, cloudy, sunny, misty week
– thanks to Jack Frost and his naughty
goblins. The goblins had stolen the seven
magic tail feathers from Doodle, the
Fairyland weather cockerel, and taken
one each into the human world. The
feathers were used by the Weather Fairies
to control the weather so the goblins were
stirring up all kinds of trouble!

Rachel and Kirsty were helping the
Weather Fairies to get the feathers
back. Without them, Doodle was just
an ordinary iron weather-vane! Kirsty's
dad had found him lying in the park
after he'd chased the goblins into the
human world. Mr Tate had brought
him home and put him on the roof
of the old barn.

"Doodle's got five of his magic
feathers back now. But I do hope we
find the last two before you have to go
home," Kirsty said, pushing open the
park gates.

Rachel nodded, but before she could say anything, there was a pattering sound and raindrops started splashing down.

The girls looked up in dismay to see a huge purple storm cloud covering the sun. The sky was darkening by the second and the rain was falling more and more heavily.

"Quick!" Kirsty shouted. "Before we get soaked!"

The girls started to run, and Rachel put her hands over her head as raindrops pelted them from all sides. She could hardly see the path ahead through the sudden downpour. "Where are we going?" she yelled.

"Let's just find some shelter," Kirsty replied, grabbing Rachel's hand and  pulling her along. "I'm soaked through already!" The girls stopped under a large chestnut tree near the park entrance. The tree's wide, leafy branches gave good cover. "Great idea," shivered Rachel, trying to shake the raindrops from her coat.

But just as she said that, there was a deafening rumble of thunder, followed by an almighty FLASH! The whole sky was lit up by a blast of lightning.

Kirsty and Rachel watched in alarm as a lightning bolt slammed straight into the chestnut.

"We need to get away from here quickly," Kirsty cried, jumping back in fright. "It's dangerous being under the trees in a thunder storm!"

"Wait a minute," Rachel said, staring at the branch. Rain was pouring off her shoulders but she didn't seem to notice. "Kirsty, look. The branch is...*sparkling*."

And so it was. The leaves were shining a bright, glittering green, glowing against the darkness of the day. Tiny twinkling lights were flickering all over the bark of the branch. It reminded Kirsty of the trees they'd seen in Fairyland – the way they almost seemed to sparkle with fairy dust. And that made her think that maybe...

"It's a *magical* storm!" Kirsty exclaimed in delight, her eyes almost as bright as the shining leaves. "Look at the sky, Rachel!"

Both girls gazed up in wonder as the lightning flashed again, and a million sparkling lights danced around the thunder clouds before fading away into the darkness.

Rachel grinned with excitement. "It's magical, all right, but very wet!" she laughed. "Let's find somewhere drier and safer. Come on!"

The Fairy Storm

The two girls charged out of the park
and back to the road. The rain was
still beating down, plastering their
hair against their heads. It was so
dark and wet that all the cars driving
past had their headlights on and their
windscreen wipers whipping from side
to side.

Rather than run all the way home, Kirsty pointed ahead. "Let's shelter in there!" she cried.

Rachel blinked the raindrops from her eyelashes as she followed her friend up the path of a large red-brick building. 'Wetherbury Museum', she read on a small blue sign.

Kirsty pulled the double
doors open and she and
Rachel tumbled inside.
Water dripped onto
the doormat as
Rachel shook
her sodden hair
back from her face.
"Phew!" she whistled.
"Talk about stormy weather!"

Kirsty was looking thoughtful.
"It must be the goblin with the
Lightning Feather who's behind this,"
she said. "He has to be close by, don't
you think?"

"Definitely," Rachel agreed. "I—"

Before she could say anything else,
she was interrupted by a deafening
ROOOAAARRR!

Rachel clutched Kirsty's arm. "What was that?" she whispered. Kirsty giggled at her friend's alarmed face. "I should have warned you — there's a dinosaur display in here," she said. "Some dinosaur bones were found in Wetherbury years and years ago. The museum has an enormous model of how the dinosaur would have looked. It roars and moves. Come on, I'll show you."

Kirsty pushed open another set of double doors that led into one of the museum galleries. A group of people were being shown around by a tour guide. Kirsty pointed to an enormous model dinosaur.

Rachel stared at the long neck, broad body and huge tail of the model. The dinosaur was standing in water that was clearly supposed to represent a river. Spiky rubber fish floated around its feet. "Wow!" she exclaimed.

Kirsty grinned. "Watch this," she said, and pressed a big red button.

The dinosaur leaned down and opened its jaws. It snapped up one of the peculiar-looking fish, then lifted up its head so that the fish tumbled down

into its belly. "That's brilliant!" Rachel said, laughing. "What happens if you press this blue button, here?"

RROOOOOAAARRRR!

"That's what happens," Kirsty giggled.

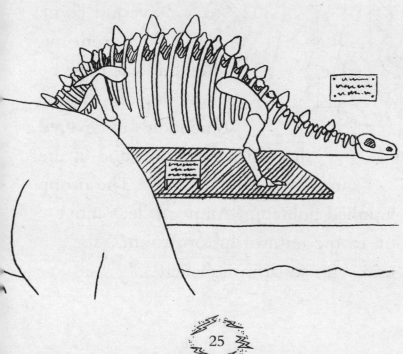

As the dinosaur's roar faded, Rachel couldn't help overhearing the tour guide. "Listen!" she hissed to Kirsty.

"…don't know where this fairy exhibit has come from," the guide was saying in a puzzled voice. She shrugged. "I've just come back from my holiday – it must be a new display. Maybe somebody's discovered that fairies were around at the same time as dinosaurs!" The group laughed politely. "Anyway, let's move on to the natural history room," she said. "It's just through here…"

26

Rachel and Kirsty
crept to the back of
the tour group to
look at the fairy
exhibit. If they stood
on tiptoes, they could
just about see over all
the heads to one of the
display cases. There seemed
to be a tiny shape in there, but they
couldn't quite make out what it was.

As the group followed the tour guide
out of the room, there was another loud
growl of thunder and the girls saw a
dazzling flash of lightning at the
windows. Once again the sky seemed
to glitter with a stream of dancing silver
sparkles. Then, all the lights went out
inside the museum.

"Oh dear, it's a power cut," the guide said in dismay as her tour group gasped. "Follow me, everyone – I think we have some torches in a cupboard through here."

Rachel and Kirsty waited until the group had left the room, then went to take a closer look at the display case. There inside was a real fairy, glowing with magic – and she was waving frantically at them!

Rachel in Danger

"It's Storm the Lightning Fairy!"
cried Rachel, hurrying to open the
case. She found a tiny catch on
the side and unlatched it so that
the glass door swung open.

"Hello, again," said Storm in
relief. "I'm really glad to see
you two!"

Rachel and Kirsty had met all the Weather Fairies at the start of their feather-finding mission, when the King and Queen of Fairyland had magically summoned the girls to ask for their help. Storm had long, straight white-gold hair and she wore a striking purple trouser suit. A golden lightning strike hung on a chain around her neck, and her purple wand sent out little crackling lightning bolts whenever it moved.

"Hello, Storm," said Kirsty, as the fairy fluttered out from the glass case. "I was wondering when we were going to see you. What were you doing in there?"

Storm tossed her hair. "The goblin with the Lightning Feather shut me in," she explained crossly. "He's somewhere in the museum. Have you seen all the lightning he's made?" She put her hands on her hips. "Please say you'll help me get the feather back. Lightning is powerful stuff, you know."

"We know," Rachel told her. "We were under a tree when lightning struck and a branch was cracked."

Storm looked horrified, so Kirsty tried to soothe her. "It was very pretty lightning, though, Storm," she said. "All shining and sparkly!"

Storm smiled. "It is beautiful, isn't it?" she said. Then she sighed. "But I've got to get the feather back before that mean old goblin does any more damage. Those goblins have no idea—"

Storm broke off in the middle of her sentence. "Someone's coming," she whispered. "It might be the goblin. Hide!"

The girls pressed themselves back against the wall and Storm swooped down onto Kirsty's shoulder. They were half hidden by a display case, and peered into the gloomy darkness. Thunder crashed again outside and Kirsty found that her heart was beating wildly. She really hoped it was just the tour guide coming back, and not the goblin. Jack Frost had cast a spell to make all the goblins bigger, so now they almost reached the girls' shoulders. As well as making the goblins stronger, it meant it was even harder for Kirsty and Rachel to get the Weather Feathers from them!

The door creaked open and the girls and Storm held their breath. It was the goblin. And to Kirsty's dismay, he was a particularly scary-looking one – with extra-narrow red eyes, long pointed ears and a thin, bony body. The lights were still out in the museum, but the goblin soon lit up the room. He was waving the Lightning Feather around so gleefully that golden bolts of lightning whizzed all over the place, crackling and fizzing, and sending

electric blue sparks shooting from everything they touched. Storm put her head in her hands. "I can hardly bear to watch," she groaned. "What does that fool think he's doing?"

"Oh!" gasped Rachel, ducking down as a lightning bolt zoomed past her head. "We've got to stop him before he does any damage," she hissed.

"Who said that?" the goblin snapped. "Fairy, was that you? Or is somebody else in here?"

Kirsty's heart pounded so loudly she was sure the goblin was going to hear it. He was turning around, looking everywhere to see who'd made the noise. At last, his red eyes fell upon the girls and he grinned a horrible grin.

"Oho!" he cried. "Planning to sneak up on me, were you?" And with a wave of the feather, he sent three fiery lightning bolts whizzing towards them!

"Duck!" cried Storm, diving into Kirsty's coat pocket. The girls threw themselves bchind a display case and the lightning crashed to the ground, missing them by a few centimetres. Wisps of glittering smoke rose in coils from a scorch mark on the floor, and the girls watched them anxiously. The smoke drifted up to the ceiling where it finally fizzled out in a shower of blue sparks like a tiny firework. Fairy lightning was certainly powerful stuff!

"What shall we do?" whispered
Kirsty, her face white.

"I don't know," Rachel whispered
back. "Storm – have you got
any ideas?"

Storm shook her head. "He's
holding the feather so tightly, there's
no way I can fly over and grab it,"
she said, frowning anxiously.

Rachel bit her lip. They needed a
plan – and quickly! "I'll just peep
out to see where he is,"
she whispered. She
poked her head
around the side
of the display
case – only to see
the goblin creeping
closer towards them.

"There you are!" he gloated and waved the Lightning Feather again. To Rachel's horror, a lightning bolt came shooting straight towards her face!

A Wild Idea

Rachel leapt back behind the display case just in time. The lightning bolt whizzed so close to her, it singed the hem of her coat.

Storm fluttered up, a determined look on her face. "Shrink to fairy size, girls!" she called. "It'll be harder for him to blast you when you're small."

Kirsty's fingers were shaking so much, she could hardly open her fairy locket. The Queen of the Fairies had given her and Rachel one each. They were filled with magical fairy dust. She finally flipped the lid open and sprinkled the dust all over herself. Seconds later, she felt the familiar whooshing sensation as she shrank smaller and smaller until she was the same size as Storm. She shook out her wings at once and pirouetted in the air. Being a fairy was so much fun!

Rachel looked like a giant next to her.
"I can't find my locket," she
said anxiously.
Kirsty gasped
as she saw it
shining on the
floor under a
display case, out
of Rachel's reach.

She pointed it out to her
friend. "It must have fallen off when
you dived for cover!" she cried.

Before Kirsty could fly down and grab
the locket, the goblin came lumbering
over. He was so close now that he
was almost next to Rachel. He
held the feather tightly in his
hand and Rachel could see
a wicked glint in his eye.

"Help!" she cried, dodging neatly to one side and running away. "Can you distract him, Storm?"

Storm was whizzing through the air, trying to get close enough to Rachel to magic her into a fairy – but the goblin was blocking her way. And he was still waving the feather around, sending lightning bolts flashing in every direction. It was too dangerous for Kirsty or Storm to get any closer to their friend.

"What are we going to do?" Kirsty wailed as she watched Rachel running away from the goblin. The doors crashed as Rachel charged into the next room. Kirsty and Storm flew helplessly behind.

This room was full of animal and insect exhibits. Luckily, Kirsty realised, there were no people around. The tour group must have braved the weather and headed for home.

The goblin was chasing Rachel past cases of colourful butterflies, and then around a large glass ant house containing thousands of bustling ants. The goblin shook the feather, and a bolt of lightning slammed against the ant house, scattering the ants from their work.

Kirsty thought her friend had done brilliantly to outrun the goblin so far, but she knew Rachel couldn't keep it up for ever. She had to think of some way to rescue her friend!

Kirsty racked her brains as she and Storm followed Rachel and the goblin back into the dinosaur room. Suddenly, she spotted a large mirror hanging on one wall. An idea came to her. A crazy idea. A wild idea! But she thought it might just work...

Kirsty to the Rescue

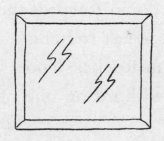

Kirsty pointed up at the mirror. "Would lightning be strong enough to break that?" she asked Storm quickly.

Storm shook her head. "No, fairy lightning isn't like normal lightning. It would just bounce back off a mirror," she replied.

Kirsty grinned. "Perfect," she said.

"I'm going to try and surprise the goblin. You get ready to grab the feather!"

Kirsty could tell from Rachel's face that her friend was starting to get tired, so she flew down towards the goblin at once. He was just stretching out a bony hand to grab Rachel's coat, when Kirsty tugged hard on one of his long red ears.

"Ow! Who did that?" he yelped, jumping back angrily.

Kirsty fluttered up in front of the mirror. "Coo-ee! Over here!" she yelled, waving cheekily. "Catch me if you can!"

She saw the goblin aim the Lightning Feather straight at her. "Cheeky little fairy," he yelled. "Take that!" And at once, another crackling, golden lightning bolt went shooting towards Kirsty.

Kirsty held her breath as she watched it whizz through the air. It was so close she could practically feel its scorching heat on her face...

53

"Move!" Rachel shouted in panic, terrified that her brave friend was going to get hit.

But Kirsty waited until the very last second, and then, just as the lightning was about to strike her, she dodged out of its way. The fairy lightning struck the mirror and, as Storm had predicted, it bounced right back — straight at the goblin!

"Help!" he shouted, trying to get out of its way. He tripped clumsily over his own feet and fell to the ground beneath the dinosaur model – dropping the Lightning Feather as he did so!

Quick as a flash, Storm was there, diving towards the precious feather in a blur of purple and gold. She snatched it up and flew high in the air, well out of the reach of goblin fingers! "Nice work, Kirsty!" she cheered triumphantly.

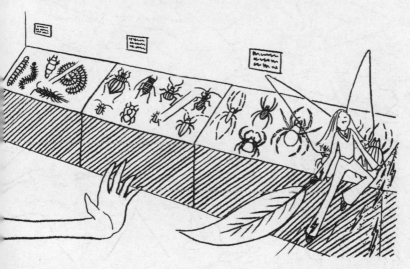

"Hey!" yelled the goblin in fury, jumping up to try and reach the feather. He fell awkwardly against the dinosaur, lost his balance and tumbled right into the water tray, with the rubber fish!

Grinning mischievously, Storm pointed the Lightning Feather at the model dinosaur. A stream of fiery lightning bolts shot out of the feather and struck the red and blue buttons on the control panel. Rachel's eyes widened in delight as the dinosaur sparkled all over for a second, and then...

"RROOOOAAARRRRRR!" went the dinosaur, opening its jaws. And with that, it bent down and snatched up the goblin in its teeth!

Doodle's Warning

Rachel, Kirsty and Storm watched in amazement as the dinosaur lifted up its head with the struggling goblin still in its mouth.

"Put me down!" the goblin raged. "Aaaaargghh!"

Of course, the model took no notice of the goblin but obediently went through its usual process. It tipped its head back, opened its jaws a little wider, and...CLATTER, CLUNK, BANG, BANG, CRASH! The goblin tumbled right down into the dinosaur's hollow belly. A furious hammering immediately started up inside the model. "Let me out!" yelled the goblin. Laughing with delight, Kirsty sprinkled another pinch of fairy dust over herself. It glittered a bright, lightning white and then she felt her wings disappear and her legs grow and – WHOOSH! – she was back to being a girl once more.

She went straight over to Rachel and hugged her. "Are you all right?" she asked. "That got a bit scary, didn't it?"

"Yes," Rachel agreed. "But we managed it, thanks to your brilliant idea, Kirsty. Now we've got Doodle's sixth feather!"

Storm flew over with Rachel's magical locket. "Here you are," she said, handing it over. "And I think we'd better leave while we can," she added nervously. "It sounds like the goblin's trying to climb out, and it won't take him long to escape and tell Jack Frost what's happened.

They could all hear the determined scrabbling sounds that were coming from inside the dinosaur.

Rachel fastened
her locket
carefully around
her neck as the
friends headed
for the museum's
exit. "I can't
believe I missed out
on being a fairy today,"
she said with a sigh. "That's
the only bad part. That – and nearly
getting blasted by fairy lightning!" she
finished with a smile.

The girls and Storm rushed out of
the museum. Outside, the bad weather
had passed, the rain had stopped and
the dark clouds seemed to be melting
away. The sun came out and made
the wet pavement glisten.

Rachel glanced down and groaned. "Oh, no," she said. "My coat! I'd forgotten it had been singed by the goblin's lightning."

Kirsty looked over as Rachel pulled up her coat hem to examine it. The material was blackened and scorched, and the stitching had frazzled away.

"Mum's going to go mad," Rachel said. "This coat was meant to last until autumn!"

"Let me see," said Storm, darting down for a closer look. As soon as she saw the problem, she smiled and gently stroked her magic wand along the hem. A trail of twinkling lights glimmered over the material, and Rachel gasped as the burned part of her coat started shimmering with a bright white light.

She blinked in the dazzling fairy glow, and when she looked again, she saw that her coat was as good as new! "Thank you, Storm," she gasped in delight. "Now Mum will never know!"

Storm winked. "I should be the one thanking you two," she said. "Doodle will be so pleased to have another feather back in his tail!"

They hurried down Twisty Lane to Kirsty's house. "There's Doodle," Kirsty told Storm, pointing to the weather-vane on the old barn.

Storm flew up to return the Lightning Feather to Doodle's tail, and the girls waited expectantly. What was Doodle going to say this time? Every time they had put a feather back before, the rusty old weather-vane had magically come alive, just for a second, and squawked out part of a message. So far, he had said, "Beware! Jack Frost will come if his...". The two friends were anxious to find out what Doodle was going to say next. Jack Frost would come if his...*what?*

As Storm carefully slotted the
Lightning Feather into place, Doodle's
iron feathers softened
and shimmered
with a thousand
fiery colours.
His head
turned towards
the girls and
his beak opened.
"...goblins fail!"
he squawked
urgently.
Then, as fast as
he had come to life,
the colour vanished from
his feathers, his head turned back
with a rusty creak, and he was an
ordinary weather-vane once more.

Rachel and Kirsty looked at one
another in alarm. "Beware! Jack
Frost will come if his goblins fail!"
they cried together.

Storm looked
worried, too.
"If you find the
Rain Feather,
then Jack
Frost's goblins
will have
failed," she said.
"That doesn't sound
good." She fluttered down
to Kirsty and Rachel. "You must be
careful, girls. Jack Frost is very sneaky."

"We know," Kirsty said, biting her
lip. "But we will be careful, don't
worry, Storm."

Kirsty and Rachel hugged Storm goodbye. They watched as the Lightning Fairy flew away into the distance – until she was nothing but a purple sparkle in the air. Then she was gone.

The girls stood in silence for a moment, both thinking about Doodle's warning. Rachel was the first to speak.

"We've nearly done it, Kirsty," she said. "But I think the last feather might be the hardest one to get back."

Kirsty nodded. "And even if we do get it, I'm not looking forward to seeing Jack Frost at all," she said solemnly. Then she squeezed Rachel's hand. "But we've outwitted him before, haven't we? I'm sure we can do it again."

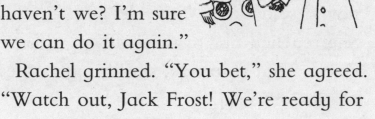

Rachel grinned. "You bet," she agreed. "Watch out, Jack Frost! We're ready for you!" she shouted.

Now it's time for Kirsty and Rachel to help...

Hayley the Rain Fairy

Read on for a sneak peek...

"I'm awake. You can stop ringing now," said Kirsty Tate sleepily. She reached out to turn off her alarm clock. That's strange, she thought, the alarm isn't ringing.

"Quack, quack, quack!" The noise that had woken her up came again.

Now that Kirsty was awake, she realised that it hadn't been her alarm clock at all. The sound was coming from outside. She jumped out of bed and peeped between the curtains.

"Oh!" she cried. There was water right up to her windowsill, and a large brown duck was swimming past, followed by five fluffy ducklings! Kirsty watched with delight as the mother duck fussed around her babies, but then she frowned.

It had been raining really hard. In the front garden, the lawn and flowerbeds had disappeared underwater. Water lapped against the walls of the old barn, and beyond the garden gate the lane looked like a silvery mirror.

Kirsty rushed over to her best friend, Rachel Walker, who was asleep in the spare bed. Rachel was staying with Kirsty for a week of the summer holidays. "Wake up, Rachel! You have to see this!" Kirsty said, shaking her friend gently.

Rachel sat up and rubbed her eyes. "What's going on?"

"I think the river must have overflowed. The whole of Wetherbury village is flooded!" replied Kirsty.

"Really?" Rachel was wide awake now, and eagerly looking out of the window. "That's odd," she said, pointing. "The water isn't so deep in the garden and the lane. How can it be right up to your bedroom window at the same time?"

"Maybe it's fairy weather magic!" Kirsty gasped, her eyes shining.

"Of course!" Rachel agreed. She knew that fairy magic followed its own rules.

Kirsty and Rachel were special friends

of the fairies. They had met on holiday with their parents on Rainspell Island, where they had helped the seven Rainbow Fairies get home to Fairyland, after Jack Frost's nasty spell had cast them out. Now Jack Frost was up to more mischief, and Rachel and Kirsty were on another secret fairy mission.

Rachel looked over at Doodle, the weather-vane on top of the barn. Usually, with the help of the Weather Fairies, Doodle the fairy cockerel would be organising the weather in Fairyland. He had seven magic tail feathers and each one controlled a different type of weather. But Jack Frost had sent his goblins to steal the magic feathers, and they had run away with them to the human world. Doodle had given chase, but without his feathers, and outside of Fairyland, he had transformed into an ordinary metal weather-vane. Kirsty's dad had found him lying in the park, and brought him home. And that's where he would have to stay, until Kirsty and Rachel could return all seven of his magic tail feathers and send him back to Fairyland...

Read Hayley the Rain Fairy to find out what adventures are in store for Kirsty and Rachel!

Meet the
Friendship Fairies

When Jack Frost steals the Friendship Fairies' magical objects, BFFs everywhere are in trouble! Can Rachel and Kirsty help save the magic of friendship?

www.rainbowmagicbooks.co.uk

Calling all parents, carers and teachers!
The Rainbow Magic fairies are here to help
your child enter the magical world of reading.
Whatever reading stage they are at, there's
a Rainbow Magic book for everyone!
Here is Lydia the Reading Fairy's guide to
supporting your child's journey at all levels.

Starting Out

Our Rainbow Magic Beginner Readers are perfect for first-time readers who are just beginning to develop reading skills and confidence. Approved by teachers, they contain a full range of educational levelling, as well as lively full-colour illustrations.

Developing Readers

Rainbow Magic Early Readers contain longer stories and wider vocabulary for building stamina and growing confidence. These are adaptations of our most popular Rainbow Magic stories, specially developed for younger readers in conjunction with an Early Years reading consultant, with full-colour illustrations.

Going Solo

The Rainbow Magic chapter books - a mixture of series and one-off specials - contain accessible writing to encourage your child to venture into reading independently. These highly collectible and much-loved magical stories inspire a love of reading to last a lifetime.

www.rainbowmagicbooks.co.uk

"Rainbow Magic got my daughter reading chapter books. Great sparkly covers, cute fairies and traditional stories full of magic that she found impossible to put down" - Mother of Edie (6 years)

"Florence LOVES the Rainbow Magic books. She really enjoys reading now" - Mother of Florence (6 years)

The Rainbow Magic Reading Challenge

Well done, fairy friend – you have completed the book!
This book was worth 5 points.

See how far you have climbed on the
Reading Rainbow opposite.

The more books you read, the more points you will get,
and the closer you will be to becoming a Fairy Princess!

How to get your Reading Rainbow
1. Cut out the coin below
2. Go to the Rainbow Magic website
3. Download and print out your poster
4. Add your coin and climb up the Reading Rainbow!

There's all this and lots more at
www.rainbowmagicbooks.co.uk

You'll find activities, competitions, stories, a special
newsletter and complete profiles of all the
Rainbow Magic fairies. Find a fairy with your name!